THE FAMOUS EXPLORERS OF NEW YORK CITY

RICHARD TAN

Giovanni da Verrazzano was an Italian **explorer**. He was born in 1485 in a small town near Florence, Italy. He worked for the king of France.

In 1523, King Francis I of France asked Verrazzano to search for a new way to China by sailing west. He wanted the spices and silk of China. **Trade** was important for France.

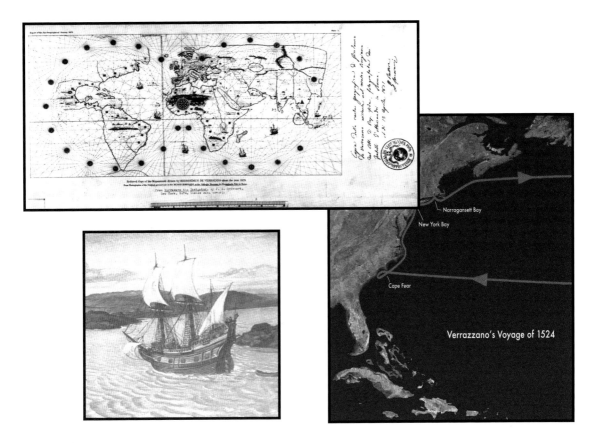

In 1524, Verrazzano's ship, *La Dauphine*, reached North America near Cape Fear. This place is on the coast of what is now the state of North Carolina.

Verrazzano sailed north. He sailed into New York **Bay**. He met **Lenape** Indians. He saw the **mouth** of the Hudson River. He thought it was a lake.

Verrazzano **claimed** the lands he discovered for the king of France. He returned to France in 1524. He died in 1528 on another **exploration**. Many people believe he was eaten by **cannibals**. New Yorkers honored him by naming the Verrazano-Narrows Bridge after him.

Henry Hudson was an English explorer. He was born in the 1560s or 1570s. In 1609, the **Dutch** chose him to be the captain of a ship called the *Half Moon*.

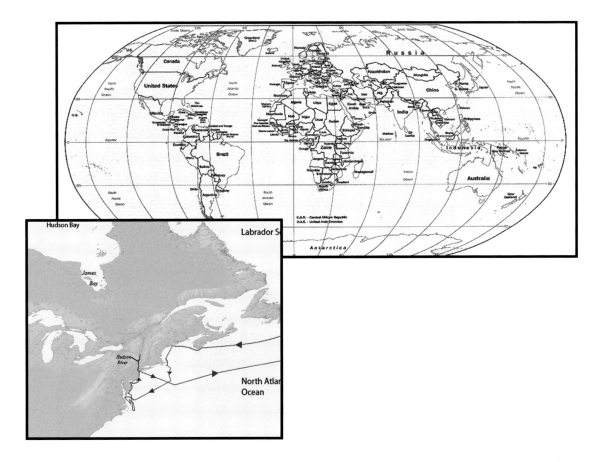

The Dutch wanted to find a new way to get to **Asia**. There were many things to buy and sell in Asia. The faster they traveled to Asia and back, the more money they made.

At first, Hudson went east. Then he went west. He sailed for months across the Atlantic Ocean. Then he sailed into the upper bay of what is now New York City.

Hudson also sailed up the river we now call the Hudson River. He saw a rich land. There were many forests and **beavers**. He met the Lenape Indians who lived there.

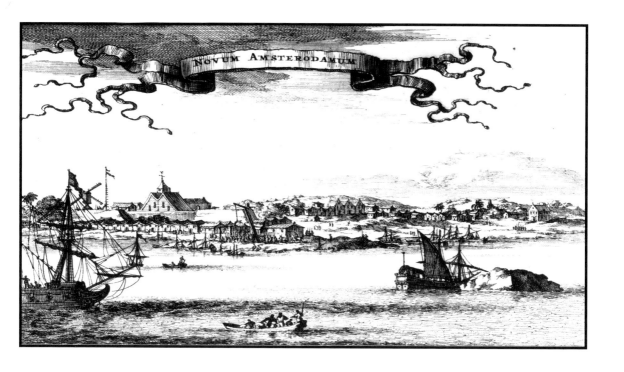

Hudson returned to Europe. He reported to the Dutch about the rich land he had found. The Dutch sent settlers to live in this new land. They made a city on the island of Manhattan. This city became New York City. Henry Hudson died in 1611.

Glossary

Asia: a large land in the East

bay: a body of water that is mostly surrounded by land

beavers: furry animals that swim and build dams

cannibals: people who eat people

claimed: said without proof that it is true

Dutch: of the country of the Netherlands

explorer: someone who travels to find out new things

exploration: a search

La Dauphine: the *Princess*

Lenape: a tribe of Indians who lived in what is now New York City

mouth: the place where a river enters the bay or the sea

trade: business